Love & Joy
COME TO YOU

ROSE CARD-FAUX

MAMMOTH CREEK

MAMMOTH CREEK

ISBN: 978-1-961245-05-1 (paperback)

For questions and comments about the quality of this book, please contact us at Admin@MammothCreekMedia.com

To all my friends who deserve better.

Note to readers:

LOVE AND JOY COME TO YOU is a story of growth and healing. While it includes some gentle references to emotional and financial abuse, sexism and misogyny, and the deaths of loved ones, I hope it manages to acknowledge the effects of those experiences without dwelling too painfully in them.

Love & Joy

COME TO YOU

To say that Cora was down on her luck would be the understatement of a lifetime. Of course, at this point, she wasn't sure she'd ever had much luck to begin with. It certainly didn't seem out of character for her that now, in the damp chill of a Friday afternoon, she was by herself in a darkish alley, digging through garbage.

To be exact, she was draped on her stomach over the lip of the dumpster behind the hardware store on her street, and she was trying to move things out of the way in an attempt to reach a perfectly usable, if oddly shaped, sheet of heavy-duty plywood, the corner of which she could see sticking up iceberg-like from beneath a sea of Styrofoam and plastic and other trash.

Before the time of the Nashes—the foster family she'd stayed with long enough for her to almost think of them as her own—Cora had made a practice of dumpster-diving. For food, for gadgets, even for clothes. It wasn't that her foster homes had deprived her, but she'd always been aware that they were temporary situations, and she'd liked the security of knowing she could provide for herself.

Today, nearly twenty years later, she supposed

her circumstances weren't entirely the same. Yes, she was digging through garbage, but she wasn't looking for food or clothes. She was looking for lumber. Or discarded construction materials of any kind.

Over the last week, in this same giant metal dumpster, she had found one salvageable pallet, a container of nails that were only slightly mis-formed, and a couple glass soda bottles in a color of green she thought she could pass off as decorative.

So far, her attempts to extricate the sheet of plywood weren't going especially well. The thing was too awkward and heavy for her to manage with just her upper-body strength. She preferred not to climb all the way into the dumpster, but she was beginning to think that was the only way she'd be able to get the plywood out.

She had just swung one leg over the edge in preparation to jump in when she heard someone at the mouth of the alley call her name.

"Cora Campbell?" It was a man's voice, curious and amused.

Cora snapped her head around, the heat of embarrassment flooding her cheeks before she even saw who was standing there. And when she did see who it was, all she could think was, *of course.*

Noah Rivera. Handsome, talented, effortlessly cool Noah. Of course, it would be him. And, of course, it would be this moment. When she was very inelegantly straddling a garbage can, her hair a mess and her backside in the air, covered only by the threadbare jeggings she'd purchased when she'd been two sizes smaller than she was now.

"Oh, hi, Noah," she said, in a voice that

pretended this was a perfectly normal situation in which to be found while her face showed that she knew very well it was not.

Noah grinned, and Cora was reminded of how pleasantly unsettling that smile had always been for her. In fact, Noah, who'd been in the Hearts of Joy community choir with her ex-husband Josh, had always had a knack for flustering her by simply paying attention when she talked.

"Care for some help?" he asked.

She looked him up and down.

He was dressed in a nice wool coat, expensive-looking loafers, and well-cut trousers that tapered down his legs, ending at the exact point on his ankles that was on trend these days. Not the sort of clothes for dumpster diving. He was carrying two coffee cups, too, which meant he was on his way somewhere. To someone.

"No—" Cora began, but he was already setting the coffee cups down on the asphalt at his feet and stepping over beside her to peer into the dumpster, too.

"You lose something in there?"

My dignity, Cora thought, but what she said was, "I was trying to get that board there." She pointed it out and then added, a little defiantly, "I almost had it." But since the board in question was still nearly fully buried in debris, she didn't think her claim seemed very believable.

Noah didn't ask why she was digging through a dumpster to get a piece of wood. He just said, "Here, let me try," and waited for her to hop back down to the ground so that he could hoist himself up and drape his own body over the dumpster's edge. From her new vantage point, Cora had to try very hard not to notice the way his pants stretched nicely around the shape of his backside and legs.

It took him only a few minutes to extricate the plywood from its sea of garbage, drag it out over the lip of the dumpster, and lower it carefully to the ground, despite the fact that, once it was all the way free, it turned out to be nearly as wide as the dumpster itself and half Noah's own height. Cora couldn't imagine why it had been thrown away since the only flaw she could see was a shallow graze mark across one side, and she could already picture at least a dozen things she could do with it.

Noah looked at the board. He looked at her. And Cora knew what he was thinking because she was thinking it, too: there was no way she was going to be able to get this thing anywhere on her own.

"So," he said, "you're taking this…where?"

"Down the street." She waved vaguely in the direction of the shop space she was leasing. "I can manage."

There was a time when Cora would've felt consuming guilt over lying about anything, but her four-year marriage to Josh had taught her the value of keeping things to herself, and this sort of minor deflection no longer felt like a lie.

The main difference between Josh and Noah, though, was that Josh had never actually been interested in other people, so as long as his jealousy wasn't involved, he had been easy to deflect.

Noah smiled wryly at her.

"You have a truck or something we can load it into?"

"Um, no. But I'm only taking it a few doors down. I can just...drag it. On the sidewalk." It sounded ridiculous even as she was saying it, and Noah's smile grew even bigger.

"How about I help you? We can both carry a

side."

Cora felt an immediate aversion to this idea. Noah had already assisted her more than she liked. "But you have somewhere to be," she said, motioning toward the two coffee cups still sitting at the mouth of the alley.

Noah glanced at them and seemed suddenly uncomfortable. "Oh," he said, his voice almost apologetic. "No. That's—it's something I'm doing to remember my mom. Gingerbread latte. Her favorite."

"Oh." Cora stared at his face as his words sank in.

She'd known his mom. Mrs. Rivera used to come to the Hearts of Joy choir practices and chat with Cora while the choir rehearsed. She'd been a warm woman with a smile like she knew all the best secrets, and if you behaved yourself, she might share them with you. She'd frequently brought Cora homemade empanadas, conspiratorially pressing bags of them into Cora's hands and saying that if they stayed at home, Noah would eat them all before morning.

"Oh, Noah. When—?"

"About three months ago, now."

In the middle of the chaos after Josh had left her. No wonder Cora hadn't heard.

"I'll make a deal with you." Noah's mouth curled into a mischievous smile. "I help you take this house-sized piece of wood down the street, and afterward, you help me drink those gingerbread lattes so I don't have to do it alone."

Panic shot through Cora's stomach. It had been so long since she'd spent leisure time with another human being that something about it felt alarming. But there was that smile of his. And the thought of him having to mourn his mom all by himself.

"All right. Okay," she said. "But we can't carry the lattes and the plywood at the same time."

Three months ago, Cora had been the proud owner of a thriving puppy school and grooming service called The Barkamentary. It had been her dream since high school to have some sort of dog-related business. A dream stemming from the moment the Nashes' black Lab, Coco, had jumped onto her bed and kept her company during her first night in their house.

However, when Josh took off with most of her money, the business—like her life itself—had collapsed. Partly thanks to the mountain of debt Josh had left in her name and partly because, for months, she'd discovered, he'd deliberately neglected to pay the rent on the space where The Barkamentary was housed.

She'd only ever agreed to leave that responsibility up to him because he'd begun to complain about every second she gave to her business, saying she was using the puppy school to shut him out of her life. Knowing that he would make her miserable until she acknowledged his concerns in some way, she'd finally compromised, and in return, he'd left her with almost nothing.

After he'd disappeared and she'd begun to realize what a mess he'd left behind, Cora hired a lawyer to make Josh give her money back—which turned out to be impossible since he'd already fled the country and his own wellness company had secretly been losing money for over a year.

Cora then tried to get out from under all the debt with the argument that she was not the one who'd incurred it. However, she and Josh hadn't had any clear delineation between his money and hers, and she'd given him too much oversight in the financial aspects of her business. She was held liable, and, in the end, she'd been forced to declare bankruptcy and give up almost everything of value that she still had left.

She refused to give up on The Barkamentary, though. So, while it had taken her several long, hard weeks before she'd finally found a building owner who would rent to her despite her recently ruined credit, she was now rebuilding her business over again by hand, gathering supplies from wherever she could scavenge them.

The new building stood only a block away from the hardware store. However, as she hauled the sheet of plywood there with Noah—one of them on each end of it, carrying it on its side so they didn't take up all the room on the sidewalk—Cora thought it felt like several miles. The combination of Noah in his stylish clothes dragging such a huge piece of wood down the street seemed to draw the eye of just about every passerby, and Cora cringed under the weight of their curious stares.

Getting it through the glass door of the shop required some awkward maneuvering, though, and Cora had to admit to herself that she didn't know how she would've managed it without Noah.

They left the plywood leaning against a wall and

went back for the gingerbread lattes. As he handed Cora her cup, Noah commented that the drinks should be just the right temperature now, and then the two of them fell into a not entirely comfortable silence.

At least, Cora was not entirely comfortable. She knew very little about Noah's personal life beyond the choir and his mom, and introducing either of those topics into their conversation risked bringing up Josh.

Noah, on the other hand, didn't seem to mind the silence. He walked along beside her, sipping his coffee and smiling at passersby with his usual ease, which Cora noted with just a touch of undue irritation.

Then it started to snow. Thick, cotton-ball flakes floated down. One landed on Cora's nose and melted immediately. She wiped the wet away just as she heard Noah chuckle. Glancing over, she found that he had his face tilted up to the sky, actively catching the flakes on his cheeks like it was a game.

"Mama loved the snow," he said. "Used to say the first snow of the year was her favorite holiday besides Christmas."

Cora looked up at the sky. It had been a long time since she'd really taken notice of the snow falling or the weather in general. Josh had sucked a lot of the magic out of life. But she had to admit that the sight of it now—the big flakes drifting white against the stormy gray background, the hush it seemed to bring over the world—was charming.

"Must be a sign," Noah declared.

"A sign of what?"

"That this was the perfect day for me to get these

gingerbread lattes," he answered, shooting a side-eye glance over at Cora that made her feel suddenly, unnervingly flushed.

3

Inside the shop this time, Cora watched as Noah looked around at what she was building. There was her partly constructed playground in bright colors, with ramps for dogs to climb on, shallow slides and tunnels, and little platforms that would eventually be home to doggie beds. There was the large activity area she planned to surround with bean bag chairs so children could come and interact with the dogs. In the very back, behind a wooden partition, she'd set up a grooming area with a stainless-steel dog bath she'd found at a bargain price through a local internet resale group.

Someday, she hoped to turn the entire back third of the space into a veterinary office, but that would have to wait until she was able to finish the veterinary degree she'd cut short when she got married.

For now, that area was covered in her tools and materials. All of it accumulated cheaply or scavenged, like the plywood today.

Cora had worked hard to put The Barkamentary together. She'd even used an anxiety-inducing amount of the meager funds she still had to pay an architect to create a plan for the playground and anything structural in the shop because she wanted to make sure it was all done right.

She knew things were looking good, but she still felt a sudden embarrassment to have Noah scrutinizing her work.

"You're opening another dog school," he said, turning to her with a grin that showed genuine pleasure at the idea.

She tried not to smile at the fact that he'd remembered this detail about her. But, then, Noah had a way of taking note of the particulars of other people's lives.

"The other school got shut down," she admitted. "So, I'm starting over again. New and improved."

"If I were a dog, I'd love this place."

She laughed, and her laugh made Noah's grin deepen, crinkling up his eyes in a way that Cora had always enjoyed.

"Well," she said, "it's not coming together as fast

as it needs to. I've got to open a week from Monday, or I might not get next month's rent paid."

As soon as she'd said it, she was embarrassed at having alluded to her financial situation, but Noah just nodded matter-of-factly, saying, "From how things look here, I bet you'll make it."

The only place to sit at the moment was a couple of large wooden crates set beside one of the display windows at the front of the shop. She and Noah perched on top of them, him nearest the window and her to his left, both of them leaning back against the wall.

They sipped their lattes and watched the people pass by on the sidewalk. Outside, the snow was falling more heavily now, lingering on the windshields of parked cars and looking like it might stick to the ground.

This time, Cora didn't mind the silence that fell between them. She figured Noah was thinking about his mom, and he'd speak up when he was ready. In the meantime, she was free to study his face without his noticing.

Noah Rivera was possibly one of the handsomest men she'd ever met. It wasn't just his defined jawline or his well-shaped lips or his smooth, amber-tinted skin—although those were definitely factors. It wasn't even his wide smile, or his big, dark eyes, or the adorable swoop of his wavy hair over his forehead. There was just something about Noah as a whole.

At the first choir practice Josh had brought her to —mostly so he could show her off—her eyes had been drawn to Noah again and again. She'd felt deeply guilty about how attractive she'd found him. Back then, Josh liked to tell her that, as soon as he'd fallen in love with her, he'd stopped finding any other women attractive, and she'd understood from the way he said it that the same sentiment was expected from her.

Josh, of course, had always been checking other women out, but at that point, when she still loved him, she'd believed his excuses. Believed that maybe she hadn't actually seen what she thought she'd seen. She hadn't realized yet that everything he said was a manipulation. That the only thing he loved was himself.

The first time Noah had spoken with her, during the refreshment hour that always came after choir practice, he'd been so genuinely interested in her as a person—in her opinions and ideas—that it had rattled her. She'd thought about it for days afterward. After a lifetime of being taught in millions of subtle ways that she was not worthy of much interest from other people, Noah's direct, unwavering gaze had made her feel almost too seen.

The fact that Josh, like usual, had left her to navigate the party by herself while he chatted up some other girl had only made Noah's attentiveness more gratifying. More dangerous.

And after that, when Noah made a point of talking to her at every refreshment hour—of drawing her into conversations with other choir members—she felt sure Josh would throw one of his fits about it. Show some sign of jealousy.

Instead, he seemed to think the only reason anyone in the choir would be nice to her was because she was his wife. Even Noah—whom Josh hated—escaped suspicion because he seldom talked to Cora alone. It was always with those groups of other people.

Which meant, while Josh frequently ranted about every petty thing he could criticize in Noah, it hadn't been on Cora's behalf. What Josh hated was how much attention Noah got from the choir's director, Ms. Nickels.

So, in the one area where Josh's suffocating jealousy over Cora might actually have been warranted, she'd been allowed a little freedom to make a friend.

Beside her now, Noah let out a heavy breath, and shifted position on his crate.

"Did you know," he started, his voice quiet, "that my dad was in a car accident when I was ten?" He glanced over at Cora, but he didn't wait for her to answer, as if he wanted to make sure he was able to get his whole thought out. "He was paralyzed from the waist down, and he ended up with a lot of other health issues that made it so he was basically bedridden. Mom had to take care of him. And me. Plus, working full-time to keep us housed and fed."

Now he paused, but Cora waited for him to go on, showing with her expression that she was listening. She thought he probably needed to talk more than he needed her commentary.

"When Dad died a year and a half ago, we were obviously devastated, but Mom also said it was her chance to finally live her life, and she wasn't going to squander it. She booked a plane ticket to Peru, and she planned out a whole Central American tour, visiting Machu Picchu and a handful of other places that she'd always wanted to see. Then," he took a little breath, "a month and a half before she was set to go—tomorrow it'll have been a year— she found out she had breast cancer. She had her first treatment a few weeks before the trip, but she insisted on still going. I traveled with her to make sure she was okay…"

He trailed off, sitting in silence for a minute. Cora hated to see him in pain. She tried to think of something soothing to say but couldn't.

"It's going to be a weird Christmas this year." He turned toward Cora. "I think for both of us."

She looked back at him, and she didn't have to wonder what he meant. Josh's disappearance had been all over the news. Of course Noah knew that the CEO of BodyWhole, the local, seemingly thriving wellness startup, was actually broke and had embezzled funds from the company and then fled the country with almost all of his wife's money. Everyone in America must've heard about it.

"Yes." She grimaced. "Yes, it's going to be weird."

"I never did like Josh, you know," Noah said with a quirk of a smile.

"Oh?" Cora raised an eyebrow.

She wasn't sure how she felt about this sudden shift from Noah's family to her own circumstances. She was supposed to be comforting him right now. That was the deal.

"Is it all right for me to say that about him?" Noah asked, and Cora at least knew how to respond to that.

"Oh, you can say anything you want about him."

"Good. Because I actually have a lot to say. It's been building up for years."

Cora laughed. "Really?"

"Well, I didn't like him in high school. He was always using people to get what he wanted. Didn't like him in business school when he was still pulling the same tricks. When he joined Hearts of

Joy choir several years back, I thought maybe he'd changed. I tried my damnedest to give the man a chance, but I couldn't like him then, either."

Cora found her smile growing as Noah spoke, appreciating the fact that someone else had seen in Josh what it had taken her too long to figure out herself.

"I forgot you two grew up together. I guess you had better instincts than I did," she said ruefully, "if you saw through him even back then."

Noah looked at her for a long minute. "You want to know when I disliked him the most?" he asked finally.

"When?"

"When he married you."

Cora's smile froze. She didn't know how to respond, or even how to read what he meant by that.

"Couldn't understand how you could possibly be happy with him. Told myself maybe he had qualities I was failing to see—"

Cora gave a bitter laugh and an emphatic shake of her head. "The best thing he ever did for me was leave."

Saying it out loud felt like a revelation. She'd been so mad at Josh—so focused on just getting through each day—that she hadn't realized how much more like herself she'd been since he left. How, for the first time in years, she felt like she could breathe freely.

"Can I tell you something else that's always bugged me about him?" Noah asked like he was about to reveal a dark secret, knocking his shoulder against hers in a way that made her catch her breath.

"What?"

"The license plate on his fancy-ass car."

Cora laughed, knowing exactly what Noah meant. "'Sperman.' *So* bad. He insisted it said 'Superman,' but I doubt anyone ever read it that way."

"Well, a man who'd name his company 'Body Hole' is capable of just about anything."

Noah couldn't stay much longer. He had an engagement with Hearts of Joy, performing at some holiday function downtown. As she walked him to the front door, he thanked her for keeping him company.

"Any time," she said, unable to keep from grinning up at him. They were standing close enough that she had to tilt her head back to meet his eyes.

"I might take you up on that," he said, and the

smile he gave her then monopolized Cora's thoughts long after he'd gone.

When Cora had found the new shop to lease, she hadn't been able to afford two rents per month, so she'd given up the rundown week-to-week apartment where she'd stayed after Josh's enormous house had been repossessed, and she'd moved into the shop herself.

She'd partitioned off a corner in the back as a

makeshift bedroom. Her bed was a sleeping bag laid out on top of a thin roll-out camping mat. Her dresser was a thrift-store roller suitcase that was missing one of its wheels. Her kitchen was a tiny microwave that sat on the ground alongside a dorm-room fridge-freezer combo.

She had found a barely adequate space heater through the trusty online resale group, and there was running water and, thankfully, an actual bathroom. It didn't have a shower, unfortunately, so she bathed herself in the doggie bath.

Before she could turn on the actual bath faucet, she had to open the water line by reaching around the tub to a spigot in the wall, which, if she forgot to turn off between baths, tended to leak water onto the floor. The bath itself was a little cramped, and the steel was always cold when she first got in. Still, overall, the tub did the job.

Cora took her time getting ready the next morning, soaking her tired muscles as best she could in the small bath. After dressing and microwaving a frozen egg sandwich for breakfast, it was time to take stock of her tasks for the day.

Her highest priority was finishing the playground. The sheet of plywood from the day before was big enough to supply everything she still needed for that. Last night, she'd traced the pattern pieces onto its surface. Today, she needed to cut them out, place the pilot holes for the screws, sand the wood where it was needed, then paint and lacquer everything.

Cora was mentally running through her list as she stepped out from the back of the shop, so it took her a minute to notice that there was a man at the store's front door.

Her heart jumped, but then she realized it was

Noah, huddled into a big puffer jacket and leaning with his back against the glass. He was looking up and down the sidewalk like he was waiting for someone. Waiting for her, probably. Because of course it wouldn't occur to him that she was actually living here.

When she unlocked the door, Noah started a little, standing up straight and spinning around. A huge grin broke across his face.

"You're here early," he said. "Talk about dedication."

"Why are you—?" She stopped when she saw an assortment of tool cases on the ground surrounding him. He was here to help.

With a sheepish expression, he said, "I don't mean to intrude, but...I could use a good distraction today."

Cora hesitated.

Yesterday, with Noah, she'd been happier than she'd felt in a long time. However, she was wary about letting anyone else into her life again just yet, and she was confused about what Noah was after. She struggled to believe he was actually interested in her, and, at the same time, she was scared by how much she wanted him to be. Still, she couldn't turn Noah away.

The two of them gathered up his tools and carted them toward the back of the shop where all her own tools were. As they set everything down, Cora saw Noah notice the sleeping bag that was her bed. Saw his gaze catch on the doggie bath, still dotted with water droplets. Then he looked at her again, taking in her still-wet hair.

Something in her chest twisted as she anticipated his pity, but it didn't come. Instead, Noah pulled off his gloves and rubbed his hands together—

possibly because of the cold, possibly as a way of showing how ready he was to work—and said, "So, what's the first task for the day?"

Cora showed him the plans the architect had made for her, and the two of them divvied up the next few steps. Noah clearly knew what he was doing with a jigsaw as he set to work cutting out wood pieces with a purpose and an enthusiasm that Cora appreciated, and he didn't complain that the only source of heat in the room was from her compact space heater.

After working for a few minutes, though, Noah asked, a little shyly, if Cora would be interested in listening to Christmas music.

When Cora didn't answer immediately, he was quick to add, "It's fine if you'd rather not."

The truth was that Cora hadn't listened to Christmas music for years now. She just hadn't had the joy for it.

"Is it something your mom liked?" she asked.

"Yes. And also me." He bit his lip and gave her a helpless look that made Cora laugh.

"How could I say no?" In fact, she was pretty sure if he looked at her like that again, she'd agree to just about anything he wanted. However… "I don't have any Christmas music on my phone, and my data is—"

She stopped herself. Yet again, she was having to bring up her financial troubles.

"Oh, I've got it covered."

With an almost childlike delight, Noah jumped up to dig a Bluetooth speaker out of one of his bags. He placed it against a wall, out of the way of where they were working, and connected his phone to it. The first song that played was "One Little Christmas Tree" by Stevie Wonder. In the past, it had been one of Cora's favorites, but she didn't bring that up.

A few minutes later, Noah began to sing along absently with the music, almost to himself, and Cora had to stop in the middle of cutting a board to look over at him. She'd forgotten how good his voice was. Rich and resonant. Comfortable in the baritone range, but with a strong, smooth falsetto.

It was strange to think she was here with Noah now instead of Josh. Not that Josh would ever have helped her with something like this. Really, it was strange to be here with anyone. She certainly hadn't expected to have any company or help.

After that, she found herself glancing at Noah more than she'd like to, as he matched up the edges of two boards or drilled pilot holes for screws. She liked how comfortable he was working near her, completing his tasks and singing to himself without needing any feedback from her.

Josh had always needed attention.

She told herself not to get too used to having someone here, though. Not to get too used to Noah.

When it was time to combine their separate pieces of plywood to make the ramp, they dragged them over to the playground area and set them up next to each other.

"Could you hold these edges together?" Cora asked, bending near to screw them in place, not thinking about the fact that it would bring her face close to his. Close enough to feel the warmth of his breath. Close enough to smell his earthy aftershave.

She had to force herself not to think about it as she worked her driver. But she wasn't very good at not thinking about it and, after putting in a few of the screws, she glanced up at him reflexively, finding his eyes on her, steady and considering.

"Have you really built all of this by yourself?" he asked. "It must've taken you months of work."

She nodded, then looked away from him, her pulse beating a little too fast.

"I learned how to build things because it was my foster father's hobby. I thought it might make him more interested in adopting me," she said, too quickly. Embarrassed to be saying it at all. "I learned to sew, too, to impress my foster mom."

She glanced up to find Noah still staring at her, and, possibly because the sympathy in his face still held no hint of pity, she went on.

"They talked about it all the time for a while there. Dangled adoption in front of me whenever they were feeling generous. I'd lived with them for nearly four years before I realized it was never going to happen. Took me another four years to fully give up hope."

"Cora," Noah said, and to hear him say her name like that…

She looked away again. Not because she was afraid of his pity anymore, but because she knew it wouldn't be there. And because the things she could see in his expression were even scarier. Especially considering the way she was feeling about him herself.

She finished the last few screws with a business-like precision, aware of his eyes watching her face the whole time.

"Well, that's that one finished." She tried to sound nonchalant.

She put the driver down and looked at him now, because she couldn't avoid it forever. His eyes were still on her, though not as intensely.

"Want some lunch?" he asked. "I noticed a deli a

few shops down."

She *was* starving. In fact, she'd been half-starving for weeks now, rationing out her food to leave more money for finishing the school. But with Noah here, and with the progress they'd made meaning she'd be more likely to open for business on time, she decided she could splurge a bit.

She nodded, and Noah grinned. With a little slap on the side of the slide they'd just built, he stood up and pulled out his phone to look up the menu. After Cora decided what she wanted, Noah offered to get the food and bring it back so they didn't lose much working time.

He even left his phone. "Keep the music playing while I'm gone," he instructed with a smile, and pointed to his smart watch. "I'm covered."

Cora's instinct was to protest, but she made herself accept his offer with a simple, "Thank you," and an answering smile.

Once he'd left, Cora threw herself into her work again, not wanting to give her mind time to dwell on him or anything she might be feeling for him. At some point, without actually deciding to do it, she began to sing along with the music. It had been a long time since she'd sung. There had been a period in her life when singing had been one of her favorite things to do, but that seemed like a very distant version of herself, so she was surprised at how much she still enjoyed it.

After "I'll Be Home for Christmas" and "O Holy Night," she let herself get fully into the music, belting out "Last Christmas" with all the force her lungs could muster.

She didn't notice when Noah came back. Didn't hear the door swing open or see him step inside. Didn't realize he was there until the song ended and he said from behind her, "Why didn't you ever sing with the choir?"

She snapped her head around, practically dropping her drill.

"How've you been hiding that voice away for this long?"

Heat rushed to her cheeks, and she stammered for a second before finally muttering, "Josh said I lacked technical training."

Noah stared at her, his jaw tight. He stood there, rigid, with the bag of sandwiches in one hand and the drink carrier in the other, looking like a formidable delivery boy.

Finally, he said, "Didn't think I could dislike that prick any more than I did already."

It surprised Cora into a burst of laughter, which brought an answering smile to Noah's lips.

"Sorry." He stepped over to her and dropped

down to sit cross-legged on the floor. "I guess I shouldn't say things like that."

"You think I'll be offended?" Her laughter was still evident in her voice as she shook her head. "Josh was awful. I only stayed with him because I'd already been taught I didn't deserve anything better."

Noah studied her face as he handed over her sandwich and drink. "And now?"

She wanted to look away, but she made herself meet his eyes as she considered his question.

"These last few months—being alone—handling the mess Josh left for me...At first, I didn't know what to do. His parents made it obvious they weren't going to help. Made me feel like it was all my fault." She dropped her eyes from Noah's. Studied the sandwich in his hands for a moment before looking back up. "The Nashes, the foster family I told you about—I emailed them, asking for some assistance, just to tide me over. Promised I'd pay it back. The only response I got was, 'Sorry you're in another mess. You sure know how to pick them.'"

Cora wasn't entirely sure why she was telling Noah all this. She was cringing a little internally as she spoke, but at the same time, she realized she wasn't as embarrassed as she thought she'd be. Noah had a way of making her feel like it was okay for her to say anything she wanted.

"Once I realized I was on my own, I didn't end up feeling as upset about it as I expected. Don't get me wrong, it hurt. It sucked. But it felt like—like I can finally just let go of all of them. I can take care of myself. Stop looking for my salvation in other people. So," she gave him a lopsided smile, "to answer your question: I can't say I know what I deserve, necessarily, but I know I won't be letting any more Joshes or Nashes into my life."

Noah kept quiet for a minute, his eyes still on her face, his expression difficult for her to read.

"Mama always really liked you," he said finally. "Dad would've loved you, too."

They worked side-by-side the rest of the day and well into the evening, ordering pizza when they started to feel hungry again. They finished the playground and started on the dog "toilet," a spot away from the activity spaces where Cora planned to train the dogs to do their business so it could be easily cleaned up. Noah laughed when she explained what it was but otherwise took it in stride.

As they worked, Noah told her more about his own family. How his dad had been an engineer before his accident, and how afterward, on his good days, he'd have Noah push him in his wheelchair out to the backyard where he had a wood shop, and the two of them would work on projects together. How Noah often had to miss out on activities with his friends because his dad would be sick and his mom would have to work. How he'd be frustrated and feel sorry for himself, but then, sitting there with his dad—watching movies or reading him books—he'd always have this moment when he'd remember how lucky he was just to have his dad there at all.

"Those are some of my favorite memories now," he said, smiling over at Cora. "Of course, the best memories were when Mom was with us, too."

When their work for the day was finished and they'd put their tools away, Noah stood in the back room, holding his bags. Cora saw him glance at her sleeping bag, then at her little microwave and her fridge. When he looked down at her, a certain tentativeness in his demeanor, she wasn't sure what he was going to say next. She held her breath.

"Would it be all right if I came again tomorrow?" he asked, his smile shy, and Cora breathed again.

"Sure." She gave a little nod. "I'd like that." And when his shy smile stretched into a gratified grin, she knew she already liked him more than she should.

The next day, Cora had planned to put together some window displays of little wooden winter dioramas with dogs and their people playing. She'd already cut out all the pieces and painted the people and the dogs. She just needed to paint the trees and the rest of the scenery.

She didn't dawdle at all while getting ready this

time. In fact, she woke up bright and early, feeling uncharacteristically bright herself. She hummed Christmas music as she took a quick bath and got dressed. She even bothered to do her hair and put on a little makeup. Not for Noah's benefit, she assured herself, but simply because she wanted to look as bright as she felt.

When Noah got there, she showed him her pieces for the dioramas, and he held a few of them one by one, studying her work.

"These are amazing!" he said. They were both kneeling on the ground next to the box of wooden people, and he looked at her over the top of it. "Where did you learn to paint like this?"

"At school. Junior high and high school. It was one of the few things I did for myself."

She was unsure how to react to someone being so openly appreciative of something she'd created, so she was relieved when Noah put the figures back and asked what she wanted him to do today.

When she suggested that he could help her paint the rest of the diorama pieces, though, he gave her an adamant and laughing "no."

"I'm good with design and aesthetics, but I wouldn't be able to match your painting skill."

"Are you a designer, then?" Cora had thought he worked in some sort of marketing position.

He gave a noncommittal nod that was practically a denial.

"That was my focus in undergrad. Now, it's only part of what I do. I'm a social media manager at an advertising firm. Actually..." He looked at her, considering, like an idea was growing in his mind. "I could do social media outreach for your dog school—"

"Oh, no." She instinctively shut him down. "I'm

not going to let you do that for me."

The vehemence in her own voice shocked her, and she felt bad when Noah's smile wavered.

"I'm sorry," she said. "It's just that Josh was so— He never gave me anything without trying to use it to control me. To make me feel like I owed him."

Noah nodded, his face inscrutable. Then he stood up with a forced nonchalance, holding out his hand to help her up, too. She took it, trying to see in his expression if he was still hurt. But as she stood, he met her gaze with a tentative, playful smile.

"I wouldn't do it for free," he said, in a tone to match his smile, as his thumb traced a circle on the back of her hand.

It sent shivers up her arm.

"And I wouldn't want gratitude," he continued. "Maybe we could work out a deal on commission, once you're making good money through the school. Maybe in the form of letting my dog attend?"

"You have a dog?"

She couldn't hide the delight in her voice, and Noah's smile grew even bigger as he shook his head.

"But I'll get one if it means seeing you more."

For a second, her heart stopped. She stared back at him, unable to decide how she should react, frozen in place by his words.

"Honestly," he went on, still smiling and shifting his hold on her hand so his thumb was now tracing the lines in the skin on her palm. "I've wanted a dog since I was a kid. Didn't seem advisable then, with my dad's situation. But now…Why don't you have a dog, by the way?"

"Oh, I—"

"Let me guess." He held up his other hand.

"Josh?"

She nodded, and Noah gave a gentle roll of his eyes.

"I've been watching the local rescues, though," Cora said, casually pulling her hand out of Noah's grip before his touch drove her to distraction. "And I plan on bringing home a dog of my own once— once my life's more stable."

"Well," Noah clapped his hands together, "let's get to work, then."

Since he was better at design, Cora asked him to assemble the window displays while she finished painting the last pieces. About midmorning, they took a coffee break, and this time, when they sat on the crates by the front window, there was less distance between them. Much less. Cora was so aware of their closeness, she thought she could measure the gap between them to the nearest tenth of a centimeter.

They reminisced about some of their shared experiences with Hearts of Joy choir—including a fair number of stories about Josh throwing fits—and Cora enjoyed laughing with Noah over the childishness of the man who had made her feel small for so long.

They finished the dioramas just as the sun was starting to set that afternoon. Stepping out onto the sidewalk, they looked in through the windows at what they had created, the golden-tinged light of the setting sun touching all of it with an almost magical glow. Noah pulled out his phone and snapped a few photos, then looked at her.

"So, how about it? Will you let me build a social-media presence for The Barkamentary?" He asked it like she'd be doing him a favor. "At work I have to do this sort of thing for clients I don't care about.

But I care about—" He stopped himself. "I'd enjoy this. And all I'd do is get it set up so that you can take it from there."

A part of Cora yelled at her to remember all the times she'd been burnt by people who'd pretended they were trying to help. But Noah wasn't trying to guilt her into it. He wasn't claiming he had any right to this part of her life. He wasn't trying to control anything. He was offering a service, and then he was leaving it up to her. If she said no, she knew instinctively that he would drop it.

But she didn't want to say no.

"Sure," she said, and was gratified by one of Noah's most infectious grins. "But," she turned to him, pressing her pointer finger into his chest and looking him firmly in the eye, "Your dog attends free. Once you've got one."

After that, Noah had to go to choir rehearsal.

They practiced and performed a lot during the Christmas season. He invited Cora to come with him, but she declined. She couldn't stomach the idea of hanging around the rehearsal waiting for Noah like she used to wait for Josh.

But as she sat alone later, eating her microwaved Cup Noodles and going over what still needed to be done before opening day, she felt Noah's absence. And she didn't know what to think about the fact that after only one weekend, she was already getting used to having another person in her life again.

Noah texted her that night, then all through his workday on Monday. Asking her about her preferences on branding for The Barkamentary. Sending her pictures of his ideas.

He came to help her with the shop as soon as he was done with work, bringing dinner with him and not bothering to keep any distance between them when they sat on the crates. Leaning in even closer as he showed her the photos he'd taken of the dioramas they'd made the day before. Asking if she'd be okay with him posting them to the social-media accounts he'd already created for the puppy school. Letting his eyes linger on her face every time she looked up at him.

The next day was much the same, and Cora found herself worrying less and less about whether this was the right thing for her right now. Every interaction with Noah was so different than it had been with Josh. Noah himself, of course, was nothing like Josh, but Cora had changed, too.

She didn't tiptoe around expressing her own feelings. If she didn't agree with something Noah said, she didn't hide it. If Noah suggested they do something she didn't want to do, she'd say so, and Noah would accept it without getting defensive or passive-aggressively trying to change her mind.

Expressing things she *did* want was a little harder —like asking him to do something he hadn't already offered, or even requesting that they turn the music on when he'd forgotten—but it got easier and easier each time she tried it out. Like building a muscle she'd hardly used before.

Sometimes, she found herself thinking, *Oh, this is how healthy relationships work,* and then caught herself on her use of the word "relationship."

On Wednesday, when Noah didn't text her through most of the morning, some of her old insecurities rose up. Maybe he didn't actually like her. Maybe he'd gotten bored.

She hated that those thoughts still sprang so readily to her mind, but she talked herself down. Reminded herself that the worthlessness she'd been taught to feel had been a lie. That Noah wasn't the sort of person to get her hopes up and then let her down. That even if Noah did change his mind, she'd be okay. She knew how to take care of herself.

Then Noah texted her shortly before noon, saying work had been chaotic that morning and asking if he could drop by and bring her lunch.

"That would be great," she texted back, and then was so distracted while she waited for him that she drilled two pilot holes in the wrong board and had to fill them in with epoxy before she could continue.

She and Noah sat on their usual crates, and, as they ate the falafel gyros he'd brought, Noah mentioned that his family had had a tradition of going to *The Nutcracker* ballet every Christmas and that sometimes his dad had even managed to attend. Noah said he'd bought tickets this year as soon as they went on sale.

"After I did it, though, I thought, 'I'm not going to want to go to that. Not this year.' And I believed that was true, but—"

He looked at Cora, his eyes both sincere and somewhat apologetic.

"I think I am going to go. It's tomorrow. Very last minute, I know, but…would you want to go with me?"

Cora's first thought was that she had sold all of her clothes that would be suitable for an event like that. Her second thought was that she still had so much to do before the opening of The Barkamentary. Her third thought was that she really wanted to go. Partly to make Noah happy. Mostly for herself.

"I'd love to," she said, meaning it, and when his

face broke into one of his wide, warm smiles, Cora couldn't help grinning, too.

As soon as he left to go back to work, she walked several blocks to the nearest thrift store and bought herself a dress, coat, and shoes for just under forty-five dollars. They were the first clothes she'd purchased for herself since Josh left.

Cora had never seen a ballet in person—it wasn't the sort of thing Josh was interested in—but *The Nutcracker* was beautiful.

Sitting there next to Noah, feeling the energy of him, the heat of his body close to hers—every moment of the ballet was underscored by his nearness. And the performance itself wove a magic that was like a tangible thing in the room.

When the ballet was over and they were leaving, Cora felt like that magic still clung to her, like an extra layer to her thrifted dress.

Noah seemed affected, too, though maybe differently than she was. She had thought tonight would be hard for him and been prepared to be his emotional support, but his quiet manner didn't seem so much grief-stricken as it did introspective.

When they stepped out onto the sidewalk, neither of them seemed to want to leave. They lingered by the entrance, leaning silently against the wall and watching everyone else coming out. The knuckles of their hands brushed softly against each other once before Noah tangled his fingers with Cora's. Her breath caught at his touch, but then she slid her hand fully into his.

They waited like that until the last of the

stragglers had left the building and the cold of the night began to seep through their coats.

"Would you—?" Noah glanced down at her, one of his tentative smiles touching the corners of his lips. "Would you help me finish the tradition with some hot chocolate at my place?"

Cora paused over what this might mean. Going to his house—his space. The intimacy of that, combined with whatever the two of them were feeling tonight. She only hesitated a moment, though, before saying, somewhat tentative herself, "Yes, I'd like that very much."

Noah's apartment was both a surprise and everything she would've expected. Each piece of furniture was brightly colored and unique, up-cycled by someone with obvious skill and an eye for design. The walls were covered with pictures of him and his parents, scattered among art pieces by some of his favorite artists, along with some graphic pieces of his own creation.

He gave her the tour, describing everything to her. The furniture he'd made with his dad. The pieces he'd done himself. There were knickknacks all over that had belonged to his mom. Some travel souvenirs from their trip to Central America and some from earlier trips before his dad's accident. In someone else's home, they might have looked tacky, but the way Noah displayed them, they seemed almost like curated works of art.

To Cora, the place was a visual representation of Noah himself, and as he guided her through it, her hand held comfortably in his and their bodies so close they bumped against each other every few steps, she began to feel almost drunk on the sheer Noah-ness of everything.

In his kitchen, he set some milk to warm in a saucepan on the stove and pulled out a bulk-sized powdered chocolate container. "Mama used to throw together all the dry ingredients for her cocoa recipe at the beginning of every fall," he explained. "She'd keep it in one of these containers so we could pull from it through the season. I made it myself this year." He gave Cora a rueful smile. "So, I can't promise it'll be as good."

Cora supposed there was nothing inherently thrilling in a man measuring out hot chocolate fixings, or in his taking time to select which mugs they'd be using, as if the choice were as important to the evening's ritual as the hot chocolate itself— but she found she couldn't look away from him.

She found, also, that she was smiling as she watched him, enjoying the little movements of his body—his tic of tapping each mug as he considered it, of scratching the back of his head as he thought. She was aware of a growing sense of exhilaration. Of an unsettling giddiness at the unlikely reality of actually being here, with him, after what her life had been the past few years.

Then Noah turned from the cupboard and caught her watching. Caught the lingering smile on her face. And he paused, staring back at her, an answering smile touching the corners of his mouth.

The air felt charged between them. Alive. And in response, it was as if Cora's body lit on fire. She thought Noah was going to step across the kitchen to her, and she knew that she would welcome it, whatever might happen then.

But he didn't. Instead, he turned back to his cocoa preparations with that smile still on his face, glancing at her again as if to let her know he'd like to close the distance between them even if he wasn't actually doing it.

Cora felt a certain amount of relief. As much as she knew she wanted Noah in this moment, she still wasn't sure she was ready to jump fully into whatever was building between the two of them, and she was grateful that he seemed to sense that.

They sat on a small couch in his living room, Noah at one end of it and Cora at the other, her body turned toward him and her legs stretched out so that her feet could rest against his thighs. Even that much contact between them felt charged. So, when Noah pulled out a photo book his mother had made the previous year of all the family's past Christmases, Cora used the opportunity to sit up and move closer to him. To lean into him as they looked over the photos.

She told herself this was as much as she would allow tonight. She would enjoy this moment with him, and then she would go home and go to sleep. And in the morning, she would think more clearly about her feelings for him.

But Cora got caught up in the alchemy of Noah again. Caught up in the rise and fall of his voice as he described each photo. In the rise and fall of his body as he breathed. Caught up in the way he seemed to welcome her into this moment as if she were a natural part of his life.

At some point, she rested her chin against his upper arm—to better see the photos in the book, she told herself—and then it felt natural enough to lean fully into him, her head on his shoulder and her knees curled against his legs. And then, perhaps because she felt more happy and comfortable than she had in years, she fell asleep.

The next thing she knew, Cora was waking up

alone in Noah's bed, her dress a wrinkled mess and her makeup smeared across her face. Based on the sun shining around the edges of the window blinds, Cora guessed it was morning, which meant she had fallen asleep so deeply last night that she hadn't even woken up when Noah moved her from the couch to his bedroom.

She groaned, pulling the pillow over her face and wishing she could die of embarrassment. It didn't help when she noticed that some of her makeup had come off on Noah's obviously expensive pillowcase. She groaned again, rolling over and sitting up.

On the bedside table, she saw a brand-new toothbrush, a travel-sized tube of toothpaste, some face wash, and face cream with a note that said, "Hope these work. Found them at the corner store. Clean towels in the bathroom."

Cora couldn't help the smile that started across her face.

This gesture from Noah didn't erase her embarrassment, but it did reassure her that he probably wasn't bothered by her unexpected stay. Deciding to accept his generosity with as much grace as she had available that morning, she gathered up all the toiletries he'd left for her and took advantage of his ensuite master bath, enjoying the best shower she'd had in months.

When she stepped into the kitchen sometime later, her dress still a mess but her hair and face clean and fresh, she found Noah making *migas* for breakfast. He grinned, his eyes lingering on her in a way that made her whole body feel hot.

"Good morning," he said.

She flushed. "Good morning. Thanks for the…all of it."

His grin widened. "My pleasure."

Sitting down at the kitchen island, Cora watched him work, and again, she felt that same sense of surreal good fortune she'd had the night before. When he was finished cooking, he prepared two plates, setting one down in front of her and taking a seat in the chair beside her.

"Eat up," he said, and they did. And while they ate, they talked and laughed as easily as if they'd been doing this same thing every day for years.

That evening, Noah had a charity performance with the Hearts of Joy choir in Cora's part of town. He invited her to come, but she declined. She was aware that if she decided to have a long-term relationship with Noah, she would eventually end up going with him to choir events. However, she still didn't like the idea of reprising her role as hanger-on.

When she expressed that to Noah, he told her, half-joking, that she could solve that by joining the choir herself.

"Ms. Nickels would love it if you joined," he added more seriously, and Cora could tell he meant it.

She shook her head, smiling so he knew she wasn't bothered. "Thanks, but I've got the opening of The Barkamentary to focus on."

In that moment, Cora had no doubt about her decision, but after returning to her building, she spent the rest of the day second-guessing it. Partly because it meant she wouldn't see Noah again until the next morning and partly because she suspected that she would probably enjoy singing with the choir if she let herself really consider the idea.

She worked extra hard that day, pouring herself

into all the last-minute details of the school. She told herself it was because she had to have everything ready to open for business by Monday, only three days away, but with all Noah's help over the last week, there really wasn't that much left to be done.

By the time the evening was beginning to turn into night, Cora found she'd finished everything. She stood in the middle of her school, looking around at what she'd created, and realized that The Barkamentary was about to be a reality again. For the first time in a very, very long time, it seemed believable that things in her life might be starting to work out.

Her overwhelming instinct in that moment was to text Noah and tell him The Barkamentary was done, but she wasn't sure if the concert was over yet. She didn't want to disrupt him.

Not being able to celebrate with him, though, made his absence that much more apparent, and she wondered again why she hadn't just agreed to go to the concert when he'd asked.

She decided her muscles could use a good soak —as good as was possible in the doggie bath. She got her towel and her travel-sized bottles of shampoo and conditioner and set them on the floor beside the tub. Then, before undressing, she bent around the doggie bath to access the wall spigot. She had to really stretch to reach it, twisting her torso at an uncomfortable angle, and she tried not to think about Noah's regular-sized bathtub in his regular bathroom that did not require contortions to turn the water on and off.

She had just got her fingers on the valve and was about to switch it on when a knock came at the front door, followed by a burst of song.

Cora shot up, smashing her head on the corner of the tub and letting out a yelp of pain. Then, stumbling backward, she tripped on her towel and nearly fell to the floor, only just managing to keep herself upright. She stayed still for a few seconds, her arms out to steady her and her heart pounding, and she wondered who in the world would be caroling outside her building.

When she stepped around the partition to the front of the school, she was already in no mood for visitors, and when she saw who was outside, she froze.

It was a dozen members of Hearts of Joy choir, singing a rousing rendition of "Here We Come A-Caroling," with Ms. Nickels at the head and Noah in the middle.

For a moment, Cora simply stood there, panicking. It was one thing to regret not attending the concert—to imagine herself supporting Noah in the relative anonymity of a crowded audience—but Hearts of Joy members were here now, encroaching on her space when she was completely unprepared for them and she couldn't hide.

Then her irritation took hold again. She couldn't believe Noah had brought them here. Had ignored her wishes, just like Josh always had.

She started toward the front door, trying to decide what to do, hating that she was in this situation. Her eyes locked on Noah's through the glass, and if the sharpness of her displeasure could kill, the man would have dropped dead.

But then, she took in the expression on his face, and she saw so much apology in it that her anger calmed a little. Noah had proven he was trustworthy so far. She could give him a chance, although he'd better have a good explanation.

When she pushed her way through the door, still eyeing the carolers a little dubiously, they were just finishing their song. And, as their last notes broke off, they burst into cheers.

"Cora!" Ms. Nickels exclaimed, rushing forward as if she were going to hug Cora but, thankfully, holding herself back. "We've missed you so much. When Noah mentioned he'd been seeing you, we all wanted to come and say hello."

Cora shot a glance toward Noah, and he mouthed a very sincere "sorry" that Ms. Nickels apparently caught out of the corner of her eye.

"No, don't blame Noah," she declared. "He really did try not to give any information away, but unfortunately for the two of you, I saw you together at the ballet last night. Holding hands."

"Oh—" Cora glanced at Noah again, like they'd been caught in something secret, and the rueful smile he gave her in return made the last of her irritation melt away.

"Now," Ms. Nickels said. "We won't intrude on you for much longer, but I wanted to let you know that we are all overjoyed that you managed to rid yourself of *that man*," she rolled her eyes, "who, Lord knows, was a trial to everyone around him. And I also wanted to assure you that, after so many years of your coming to nearly every rehearsal and every refreshment hour and practically every event we ever had, we consider you one of us. None of us knew how to get hold of you after we heard the news, but you are forever part of the Hearts of Joy family, and we are here for you whenever you may need us."

Cora didn't know what to say. Ms. Nickels's speech was almost more disarming than her hug would've been. The words surprised and comforted her, but she had no idea how to show that.

She stammered out a "thank you," and then Ms. Nickels, as if sensing that this whole exchange had already been a lot for Cora, said that they'd better be on their way.

"Noah, I think we can handle the rest of the caroling without you," she said, tilting her head in Cora's direction and raising her eyebrows at him in a not-so-subtle hint. "Unless, of course..." She pinned Cora with a questioning look. "Would you like to come with us, dear?"

All eyes turned on her, and Cora froze in place again.

She looked over the other Hearts of Joy members, people she'd known before only in her role as Josh's trophy wife. But as she took in their expressions, their smiles eager and welcoming, she couldn't think of any reason why she should keep hiding herself away. She had to stop letting the specter of Josh keep her from things she knew she'd enjoy. From these people, whom she now realized she really had missed this whole time.

It was the expression on Noah's face that decided it for her, though. His eyes gently hopeful. His sympathetic smile offering her a way out.

"Okay. Yes," Cora said, and when everyone cheered again, she couldn't help laughing. "Let me just get my coat."

As she turned to step back into the building, her eyes met Noah's, and she gave him a smile that was just for him. A smile that she hoped expressed how much she appreciated him.

Cora had not been wrong in her suspicions that she would enjoy singing with the choir. Admittedly, caroling was a little different than an actual performance, but walking through the winter evening next to Noah, singing together with people who took as much pleasure in it as she did—just being with other people again—was nice, and she found she didn't feel the need to disappear like she normally did.

It was gratifying, too, when Ms. Nickels took her aside at the end of the night and asked her if she would please, for the love of all that was good and holy, stop hiding her talent away and join the choir herself.

When the caroling was over, and everyone else had drifted off to whatever they had going on that night, Cora and Noah found themselves walking hand-in-hand along the street back to Cora's place, laughing about the evening's events.

Noah apologized again for springing everyone

on her, and Cora waved it away, smiling.

"I know there's no stopping Ms. Nickels once she gets an idea in her head," she said. "Honestly, I'm glad you all came."

A woman was approaching, walking a golden retriever dressed in a knit sweater and winter booties, and when the dog pulled at its leash to try and greet Cora and Noah, the woman called out, "Don't worry! He's friendly."

That was all the invitation they needed. The two of them bent down to offer him proper greetings, and as they cooed over the delighted animal, Cora met Noah's eyes and smiled.

They didn't keep the golden retriever and his person stopped in the cold for long. After a few more adoring pats for the dog, they wished the woman a good evening and went on their way again.

"What do you think?" Noah asked in a low voice, bumping his hip playfully against Cora's side. "Should we get a golden retriever?"

Caught off-guard by the question, Cora laughed, leaning into him and shaking her head. "There aren't any retrievers up for adoption on the rescue sites right now."

She noticed she didn't feel any alarm at the assumption of their possibly having a future together, and she suspected Noah noticed that, too.

"Well," he said, "we'll just have to look at what dogs they do have."

As they approached the front of her building, near where Noah's car was parked, he invited her back to his place again, and she didn't hesitate this time.

"Yes," she said. "Yes, please."

This time, too, Noah did what he hadn't the

night before. In the warmth of his apartment, as Cora slipped her coat off her shoulders, he closed the distance between them. Stepped in close behind her and bent down to brush his lips softly against the back of her neck. It was so light that it barely counted as a touch, but it sang across Cora's skin.

She turned around to face Noah, and she found him watching her, the intensity of his gaze showing that he wanted her even as he waited to see if what he'd done was all right.

In response, Cora took his face in her hands and pulled him down to her, melting her body into his body as she pressed her lips against his. And she knew, in this moment, that she was making a good decision. She trusted Noah.

But, more importantly, Cora trusted herself.

ACKNOWLEDGEMENTS

I am incredibly grateful to the many people who bring love and joy into my life. My kids, who fill our home with laughter and magic. My Jordan, who fills my heart with the same. My family, who cultivated my appreciation of good stories. My friends, who have been my sounding boards and have trusted me enough to make me theirs. My beta readers, particularly, Mary, who helped me see exactly what Cora and Noah's story needed. Thank you to my sensitivity reader, Neff. Your feedback was invaluable. To Passant, for bringing Noah and Cora to life in your beautiful art. To Kelia, for your excellent editing skills. To Mine, Melinda, and Michelle, who each, in your own ways, have helped me understand what makes for healthy relationships and a healthy me.

*Keep reading for an excerpt of Rose Card-Faux's novel **LESSER DEMONS**, out in ebook and print now.*

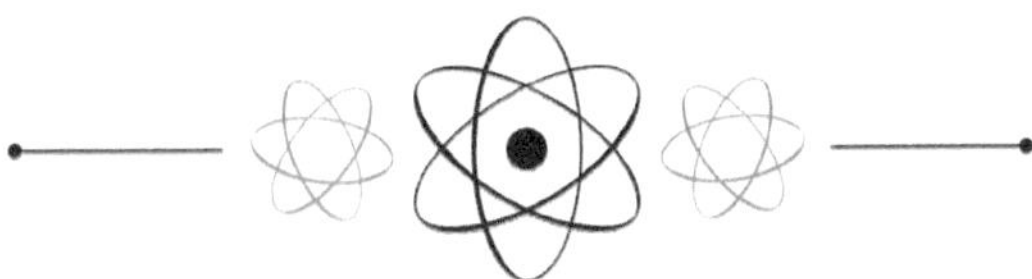

"Okay," I say, and Rishi's eyebrows rise.

"Okay…you'll come with us?"

"Well, I'm going to try to be this Way Reader thing. So…okay to whatever that means, I guess."

Up in the driver's seat, I hear Dylan let out a breath as if he'd been holding it in for years.

"Well, then," Rishi snaps his fingers. "We have no time to lose."

He swings himself around in his seat more quick than a man his age and length should be able to.

Then he and Dylan get out of the car and move to the trunk to start unpacking whatever it is they've got in there.

Mom's looking like she's been turned to stone. A human statue. All bent forward with her head against the seat in front of her, her right hand resting on her knee and her left hand cold in mine. She's still as still as still. For a second, I'm sure I made the wrong decision—that she thinks I'm making a huge mistake—but then she's turning toward me, and grabbing my other hand in hers, and pulling me around to face her more direct.

"I'm so proud of you," she says, her eyes real fierce. "You are so kind and clever and strong."

She tucks my hair behind my ears, cups my chin in her hands like she's trying to memorize me.

"You are everything you need to be to succeed. When things feel hard, remember that I know this about you, and remember that I love you, and that we'll be together again soon."

She opens up my hand and presses the broken locket into it.

"Remember that your father also loves you, even if he's gone. He saw into the future, and he knew what he had to do to protect you. You're not alone in this. You're never alone."

Over her shoulder, I see Rishi approaching her door, but she beats him to it. Rips her hands from mine and launches herself out of the car before either he or I can say anything. The cold air rushes in at me, stabs at my skin as I sit there suddenly vulnerable and alone. I'm trying to recapture some of that certainty I had a few minutes ago, but it's hard to say goodbye to your mom and still feel like some all-powerful being.

When I get out of the car, Mom's talking quiet

with Rishi off to one side. The snow's still falling, and it's cold enough that, with every word they speak, their lungs puff out steam like tiny ghosts in the night. Rishi asks her if she's got somewhere she can go where she can hide for a while.

"I have a brother in Arizona," she says, which is news to me. She's never talked much about her family, and she's got to know this comes as a surprise, but she doesn't even glance in my direction. I guess she's retreated back into her forcefield again.

Real quiet, Dylan steps up beside me and hands me my backpack. I look up to thank him but have to snap my eyes back down again right away. His face is so full of sympathy, you'd think he was trying to make me cry.

"The car's number plates are changed," he tells Rishi, who nods and walks over to the sedan without looking away from Mom.

"You can take our vehicle," he says, placing a hand on the hood. I watch as white pigment spreads away from his fingers and across the surface of the car like a never-ending milk spill. "It's practically a non-entity, and they shouldn't be able to track you."

"You'll need to lend me your cell phones too," Dylan says to Mom and me. "I'll make sure they're untraceable, and I'll hold onto them until you're not in hiding anymore."

He hands Mom a new one that's simple and black.

"Turn this on once you reach your brother's house, but don't use it until you hear from me. We will contact you as soon as we're sure it's safe."

He takes our phones over toward the tree line to a pile of things he and Rishi have pulled from the trunk. I'm wishing now I'd left my phone on during the car ride to see how my friends responded to my text. To say goodbye to them in a way that actually counts.

"It might take us some time to reach our destination," Rishi's telling Mom. "Probably a few days. Possibly more than a week. The distance is not so large for us, but there will be people looking for her, and we will have to weave our way around them."

After everything they say, Mom just nods. Then Rishi's handing her the car keys and wishing her a safe journey, and the time for her to leave is suddenly staring me right in the face.

She turns to look at me finally. Only, now I don't know what to do with it. When she comes toward me, opening her arms, I'm afraid I won't be able to hug her back. Afraid my own arms'll just hang limp at my sides and my tongue won't be able to tell her I love her. It's an instinct, though, wrapping my arms around Mom. A reflex programmed into me by years of doing that exact thing. And even if the only word I can get out is a goodbye, I think she knows what I mean.

I follow her around to the driver's side and watch as she gets into the car. The sound of the engine starting up is jarring in the quiet night. We lock eyes through the window, put on brave faces for each other so we both don't break.

"I love you," she mouths through the glass, and then, with a tight-lipped little smile, she faces forward and puts her foot to the gas.

It doesn't take long for the nearest bend in the road to swallow up the lights of the car, but I keep standing there staring after her for a while. The wind's gusting snow around my head. With a blink of my eyes, I imagine it sweeping me up and taking me along with her.

Rishi steps up beside me, puts his hand real gentle on my shoulder and considers the point on the horizon where Mom just disappeared.

"We have to leave now," he says. "We have a long way to go, and we should get started before the takers have a chance of finding us."

I just nod. The things going through my head are not the kind that feel better by sharing them.

Over by the line of trees, Dylan's messing with a tangle of straps that looks a lot like a harness.

"We've got to go by foot," he says, looking over at me. "But you can't do it the way we do yet. You'll have to ride on my back."

He holds up that harness thing, and it takes me about one second to figure out what he really means by that.

"Oh no," I say. "There is no way."

"You won't be able to keep up with us on your own. No matter how hard you try."

"I'll hang on tight. I'm not riding in some baby backpack."

Again, there's this moment where I could swear he's going to smile, but then he doesn't.

"Having you ride on my back is not exactly the most exciting thing for me either, but it's the best option we've got right now," he says in a voice that does not make me any more eager to comply.

"We will be going for hours at breakneck speeds," Rishi chimes in. He's methodically slipping items from the pile into a hiking backpack. I see a few silver emergency blankets folded up, a long-nozzled electric lighter, and what looks like a tiny brick of slate or something. "I'm afraid your flaring—your discomfort—is only going to grow worse for you, and holding tight will not be an option for long. Dylan needs to focus on his movements rather than on making sure you don't fall off. I know the situation is quite preposterous, and I would certainly feel similarly, but this is the best solution."

I don't know how to argue with Rishi on any of that. I don't think he's the sort of person you do argue with. Still, I feel about two years old as Dylan packs me into that harness. It doesn't help that, as he's doing it, I notice again how, even with that dumb beard, he's annoyingly handsome.

"Why were you rubbing yourself all up against me at the hot chocolate stand?" I ask him, and for a second, his hands go still.

"There was no such thing as rubbing," he says. "I was simply attempting to confirm the flaring was coming from you."

He's got to know I'm only goading him but, still, as he moves up to work on the strap running right under my bust line, he keeps his eyes real carefully leveled on a point just around my belly button and not a centimeter higher. From this angle his lashes are almost startlingly long, and I can't help relishing the idea that I've managed to make him a little uncomfortable. He's so pretty, it'd be easy to forget he's human.

Once I'm in the harness, he's got to strap it on himself. There are some loops hanging off the front of me, and he crouches down a bit and backs up to me to slip his arms through, buckling the harness across his own chest and waist. I stare hard at the sky the whole time he's doing this and try to pretend like it's not actually happening.

Then he stands up and lifts me into the air, and I'm pretty sure this is the most embarrassing moment of my entire life. I'm dangling off his back as stiff as a board, trying to touch him with as little of my body as possible. And I sort of hate Rishi for looking over just now and so obviously wanting to laugh at us.

"If you don't relax it's going to make things rather difficult," Dylan says.

I can see what he means. He has to bend far forward just to keep the balance right between us.

"If you wrap your arms around my neck, it might help," he prompts. But when I do, it brings my face right up next to his, and boy, does he smell good. Kind of sweet almost, and also kind of musky.

He grabs my legs at the knee and pulls them forward around his torso so he can stand straight while bearing my weight. Wrapped around him like that, real aware of the unsettling solidness of his body against mine, a new electric tingle ignites all down my arms and my legs—pretty much anywhere I've got skin. And I pray to any power that may be listening that, unlike the flaring, this is not a thing Dylan can feel.

Rose Card-Faux is a writer, an award-winning filmmaker, and maker of other things. She grew up in a house full of books and with a mind full of stories. As a child, she often blurred the lines between stories and reality, weaving tales for her friends about goblins living under their houses or butterflies actually being fairies in disguise.

She currently lives with her husband and two adorable children in Las Vegas, where she still weaves tales full of magic. In her free time, Rose likes to sew her own clothes, study languages, play piano, eat delicious food, and laugh uproariously with friends.

Find Rose on the web:
rosecardfaux.com
Instagram at @rose.cardfaux
Twitter and TikTok at @rosecardfaux

www.ingramcontent.com/pod-product-compliance
Lightning Source LLC
Chambersburg PA
CBHW021331060726
47591CB00006B/1973